FULL SPEC

YOUR POWERFUL KEY TO ABUNDANT LIFE AND TRUE JOY

WILL YOU BE HIS VALENTINE?

Ben R Peters

Foreword by Cristina Baker

Full Spectrum Love
@2024 by Ben R. Peters

Author grants permission for any non-commercial reproduction to promote the Kingdom of God. All rights reserved.

Published by
Kingdom Sending Center
P.O. Box 25
Genoa, IL 60135

www.kingdomsendingcenter.org
ben.peters@kingdomsendingcenter.org

Print edition ISBN: 9798877104006

All scripture quotations, unless otherwise indicated, are taken from the New King James Version ©1982 by Thomas Nelson, Inc. Used by permission. All rights reserved.

Cover design by Jess Seiler.

ACKNOWLEDGEMENTS

As always, producing a book requires more than an author to write a story. It takes a team to get it into your hands. I am always incredibly grateful to the amazing people in my life who have helped me do what I have no skill to do on my own. So let me mention those to whom I am most beholden:

1. First of all, I owe everything I have and everything I have ever accomplished to God, my Heavenly Father, to Jesus, my Lord and Savior, and to the Holy Spirit, whose precious gifts have the sole purpose of glorifying God and exalting Jesus Christ.

2. How could I ever adequately thank my own sweet Valentine, Brenda, for teaching me so very much about Full Spectrum Love through her beautiful example over the past fifty-six plus years? What a

wonderful blessing from our Heavenly Father she has been to me! Our love grows deeper every year we spend together, and she has truly become my one and only Valentine on this earth.

3. My amazing editors and publishing team Carole and Bruce Robbins are able to transform my rough manuscript into a masterpiece. They also go through tons of red tape to make it available to you, which is no small accomplishment.

4. And finally, we are so grateful for our spiritual daughter, Jessica Seiler, who is an awesome computer graphics specialist. We love the beautiful book covers she has created for our projects! We also love her heart to worship and serve God.

CONTENTS

	Foreword by Cristina Baker	1
	Preface	6
Chapter 1	The Problem With Love	8
Chapter 2	Love Is Love ? ? ?	12
Chapter 3	Male Love Vs Female Love	22
Chapter 4	Full Spectrum Love In Creation	27
Chapter 5	Awesome Results Of A Full Spectrum Prayer	36
Chapter 6	The Plan, The Cross, And The Blood	54
Chapter 7	Full Spectrum Romance	64
	About Ben R Peters	I
	More Books by Ben R Peters	II

FOREWORD

Just like Ben and Brenda Peters are, this book, *"Full Spectrum Love,"* is a gift from Jesus to the Body of Christ. But before I talk about this incredible book that will make you fall in love with Jesus all over again, I want to share about how I met the author of this book and his beautiful bride.

It's been over a decade since I picked up a book titled *"God is so God"* by Ben and Brenda Peters. I had no idea who the authors were, but the Lord led me to this book through a series of very unusual circumstances, which we often encounter in our walk with the Holy Spirit. As I journeyed through their story, something supernatural began to happen. Faith began to arise, and fear dissipated in us, as we heard the testimonies of this couple and their five children and how they had followed the voice of God in the most impossible situations!

God was calling my husband and I to do the same. By the time we finished reading this book, we packed up everything we owned into our SUV, along with our 7-year-old son Evan and our two dogs, and we moved to Northern California where the Lord had called us.

Shortly after we arrived, my husband was talking with a young man after a church service, and I overheard him saying that his parents traveled the United States and were itinerant ministers. There was something about the way he was describing them that made his story sound very familiar. Immediately, I asked him who his parents were, and he responded Ben and Brenda Peters! God is truly SO God!

The very next week, a young lady stood behind me in a church service and tapped me on the shoulder. She said that she had never done this before, but she heard the Lord say that we were going to become very good friends. I felt such a strong witness from the Holy Spirit when she said this, and instantly, we became the best of friends. Her name is Andrea Smith, and she is the daughter of Ben and Brenda Peters. I didn't put two and two together until much later, but what a

Foreword

testimony to the love of God and how He orders our steps like Proverbs 3 promises.

One of the things that I love about the Lord is how He divinely orchestrates our every step and move. Even when we may not know it, He is weaving every piece of our lives together into a beautiful tapestry. I wanted to share this testimony with you because this was a moment in our lives where God revealed His love to us in a way that changed us from the inside out. We had taken a huge leap of faith after reading this book, only to find that God had this very family waiting for us at our destination, and they would become family to us and display God's love for us. What an awesome God we serve, and what an adventure He takes us on when we choose to be His!

We are living in a world where love is being defined by experience and personal beliefs, but what is love from God's perspective? These are some of the questions you will get to answer for yourself as you read the pages that follow. And it will lead you to dig deeper into the Scriptures and into the heart of God, as you learn what love really is. Truth is not relative, and neither is love. Only the God *of* love, who *is* love, can define for us what love really is.

Full Spectrum Love

As I turned the pages of this book, I was reminded of the depth of His great love for me that rescued me from the gates of hell as a former atheist and addict. It is the love of God revealed through Christ Jesus that will bust down every door and wall that hinders His love from reaching each and every one of us!

My prayer for you is that as you journey through "Full Spectrum Love," the love of Jesus will encounter you like never before. Whether you've been walking with the Lord for a day or many decades, this book is for us all. It is a book for the times that we are living in as we await the second coming of our Beloved, Jesus Christ. This book will put a fire in the depths of your spirit for Jesus, and a deep desire for others to come to know Him as the God of love.

Ben and Brenda Peters have an anointing to bring the Scriptures to life, not just through their books, but in their everyday lives. Our family has been greatly blessed by the Lord through them over the years. We often wonder where we would be if God had not brought them into our lives at the time that He did. We are so thankful for His love!

I am confident that as you read this book, you too will receive an impartation of faith from the Lord to believe

Foreword

Him for the impossible because of His great love for you!

Cristina Baker

Author of
"Hope in 60 Seconds"

Speaker

Video Creator
On Social Media

PREFACE

WILL YOU BE MY VALENTINE? What a sweet and fun practice we used to participate in as kids every February 14th. Exchanging Valentine's Day cards was perhaps a very shallow expression of something we call love, but at least it was a way to focus on that wonderful entity in a special way. This practice began in the days of the persecution of Christians by the Romans. According to Wikipedia, Valentine's Day "originated as a Christian feast day honoring a martyr named Valentine, and through later folk traditions, it has also become a significant cultural, religious and commercial celebration of romance and love in many regions of the world."

Saint Valentine is alleged to have performed miracles, such as restoring the sight of his jailor's daughter. Tradition also has him performing marriages for Christian soldiers who were forbidden to marry by the

Preface

Roman emperor. Before his execution, it was said that he wrote the jailor's daughter a letter signed, "Your Valentine" as a farewell to her. And thus, we have the tradition of asking friends to be our "Valentine."

Little did we know, as kids, that we were implying that we were willing to die for our faith. But then, who can understand the depths of true love that God imparts to our human hearts? As I grow older, I'm learning how little I know in that area, as in others. I pray that in the pages that follow, we'll all come to a great and more practical understanding of the kind of love that God has to offer His children, His most precious creation.

Thus, let's ask ourselves the question: Will I be His Valentine?

CHAPTER ONE

THE PROBLEM WITH LOVE

Ask a small child to define love and chuckle at their responses. But then ask almost any adult to do the same and watch them struggle to define this very common word. They know it's more than hugs and kisses, but how do you actually define it?

The world is searching for love, but few people really know what they are searching for. If they've lived awhile on this planet, they probably have been severely disillusioned more than once, thinking they had found love, only to be devastated by the brevity of its longevity. What felt like pure, powerful, and genuine love not so long ago, now feels like a sharp, painful knife to the heart.

That's the problem with love. We think we know and understand it, but we can't define it and we can't control it. It's like the gentle breezes that refresh your soul suddenly turning into a stormy tempest that has you running for shelter. What is this chameleon-like entity that we crave and pursue, until we decide it's just not worth the trouble, and put a shell over our hearts to protect us emotionally from any more devastating pain?

Will this book give you all the answers regarding the love questions? Probably not, but I believe it will give you a greater understanding of the length, width, and depth of love, until you see its full spectrum and realize that love is a much broader concept than you've ever thought it to be.

For example: when we settle for artificial light in its usual commercial applications, our bodies may suffer because they need more of the spectrum frequencies found in natural light than those products supply. When we settle for limited spectrum love, our soul and spirit may suffer from the lack of heavenly frequencies in the love spectrum that God intended us to enjoy.

The problem with love is that our experiences often dictate our definition or understanding of love. And thus, we have a very limited concept and perspective of this wonderful gift from God. Even the ancient Greeks had more discernment and understanding of love than modern westerners, as evidenced by the different words for love in their language. They had at least three different words for the different kinds of love, which we will deal with in a future chapter.

Our greatest and most important understanding of this word "love" comes to us from God's written Word. We must understand and acknowledge the ultimate source of love before we can truly understand the full spectrum meaning of this word. God Himself is love, according to John the Beloved. Therefore, if God's essence is love, we need to find out more about Him and how He manifests that love.

One current manifestation of the "Love Confusion" phenomenon is the mantra of a certain segment of modern society. "Love is love," they proclaim and declare. What is our answer to this self-evident statement? How can we deny that love is love? It's a meaningless statement and yet it means so much to those who don't understand the full spectrum of love. We will pursue an understanding of where they have confused one frequency of love with another. It's like saying, "Light is light." It's a true statement, but commercial light is not the same as full spectrum natural light. And soulish love is not the same as Full Spectrum Love.

In the chapters ahead, we will look at the love spectrum from several perspectives, such as from physical to spiritual and from natural affection and compassion to supernatural and sacrificial love for a man's enemies. We'll examine the spectrum of love manifested in the blood of Jesus that was demonstrated by His death on the cross. And, of course, we'll examine the maturity of love in marriage and other close relationships.

Our ultimate purpose is to learn how to apply a fuller spectrum of love to our individual circumstances, however difficult they may have become, and to enjoy the fruits of such love that will be an example and a testimony to others in our sphere of influence. Love never stops with our own personal good feelings. It always finds ways to give to others and lift them up to a higher place of fulfillment and spiritual authority for the sake of the One Who is Love Personified, Jesus Christ.

With this brief introduction, let's embark on this mission to understand Full Spectrum Love more fully.

CHAPTER TWO

LOVE IS LOVE ? ? ?

"Love is love?" What a totally meaningless statement! And yet, for a certain segment of society, it is the basis for the justification of their blatant violation of traditional and biblical norms. Those who parrot this empty mantra are a prime example of the public lack of understanding of the full spectrum of love.

Let's take a look at some facts that these confused folk are missing. Our New Testament scriptures were given to us in the Greek language. In many cases, the Greeks were more exact in their choice of words, giving us a more full spectrum meaning. This is significantly true in the case of the word "love." Searching the internet, I found seven Greek words and one Latin word for love on the website: dictionary.com. Let's take a look at the different meanings of the following eight words and see why the statement "Love is Love!" is so meaningless. The first three words are the most commonly used in Scripture:

1. **EROS** (Greek)
   This root word deals with physical or sexual love, and it's used in many modern English words, such as erotic or erotica. Those words today can refer to "adult" books and videos, and they often feature photos or actions that we would consider obscene. However, I want to make it clear that eros love isn't evil or bad in its intended purpose, which the writer of Hebrews emphatically states in Hebrews 13:4a: *"Marriage is honorable among all, and the bed undefiled."* This is important to note, because if we want Full Spectrum Love, we need to understand the importance and the wonderful blessing that eros love can provide us.

2. **PHILIA OR PHILEO** (Greek)
   This word describes the love expressed in true friendship, often called "brotherly love." The meaning of "Philadelphia" is the "City of Brotherly Love." Plato, a Greek philosopher, taught that

friendship love was superior to sexual love. It could also be defined as comradery.

3. **AGAPE** (Greek)
   This is the word for love used most frequently in the New Testament. It speaks of God's sacrificial love and the love that Jesus encouraged His disciples to have towards each other and even their enemies. It's the love that sent Jesus to the cross to die for us when we were still sinners. For believers in Jesus, it's certainly the highest level of love that we can aspire to. At this point, I would suggest that, although we have been given access to God's supernatural agape love, we can never fully grasp or achieve its ultimate end. God's agape love is infinite, and we will spend eternity pursuing our understanding of it.

4. **STORGE** (Greek)
   This word is used to describe the love of family members for one another. This ranges from a mother's deep love for her newborn to the love of children for their grandparents and every other existing family relationship.

5. **MANIA** (Greek)
   This is an evil form of attraction and isn't true love. It's the passion of a stalker to attack his victim. It's a madness of many varieties. It's not a type of love

that belongs in our definition of Full Spectrum Love. It's the most selfish and perverted form of attraction, often confused with true love.

6. **PRAGMA** (Greek)
   This is referred to as practical love. According to dictionary.com, it's doing the right thing based on "duty, obligation, or logic." It would apply to the world of "arranged marriages" and other non-romantic arrangements, bringing people of the opposite sex together for financial or other practical reasons. I imagine it could also be applied to what is commonly called "Tough Love."

7. **PHILAUTIA** (Greek)
   This word refers to a person's self-esteem or respect for themselves and their own body and personality. This type of love can be positive or negative, with the extreme becoming egomaniacal or narcissistic.

8. **LUDUS** (Latin)
   This word means playful love, which can involve flirting, seduction and casual sex, and the pursuit of a non-committal relationship. Again, we would not include Ludus in our full spectrum of Christian love.

With these various definitions of the many varieties of passions or activities referred to as "love," we can see more clearly the ridiculousness of the meaningless statement "Love is love."

Yes, of course, love is love. But which definition of love are you using in the first word of the statement, and which are you using for the last word?

What they are trying to say is that EROS, MANIA, OR LUDUS IS PHILEO OR AGAPE. In doing so, they have confused many people and are in tacit agreement with them. After all, it's like the mathematical statement that $X = X$, which is true. But to be honest, they are really saying $X-1 = X-3$, and that is not a true mathematical statement. It's a deception designed to justify breaking God's perfect law, which was given to keep us happy and prosperous both as individuals and societies.

PRACTICAL APPLICATIONS FOR BELIEVERS

If we want to pursue the benefits of true Full Spectrum Love, we must be open to growth and the expansion of our expressions of that love. Let's start with the kind of love that gives humans the most trouble – eros love.

Eros love, when defined simply as physical or sexual love, is a precious gift from God our Father. We are obeying God's first command that He gave to Adam and Eve when we are fruitful and multiply. Eros love is also a wonderful and pleasurable way to bond with our marriage partner, enriching and blessing most couples over several decades.

There are many psychological and physical benefits of sexual love. This data is well documented and can be researched on your own. Conversely, let me add this to all the valuable data: the devil only perverts what is, in itself, a good thing. He comes to steal, kill, and destroy. He wants to steal God's precious gift from you and your spouse by any means possible. He wants to kill your natural affection with perversion, so you can't enjoy the blessings of this gift. And finally, the devil wants to destroy your fruitfulness and Christian testimony by every means possible.

If you want the blessings of Full Spectrum Love, please pursue a healthy and God-honoring sexual lifestyle. You may feel like you have been made differently and it's not possible for you to abide by God's precepts. But God has not set you aside or forgotten you and your individual needs. He is a God of the impossible and He can reverse what His enemy has done to you. You are not a mistake. You have been ambushed by the enemy. He came to steal, kill, and destroy you and your ability to be a witness of God's goodness. In

Jesus' name, I take authority over the insidious lies of our adversary and declare you free to pursue God's righteousness and justice for the rest of your life.

MORE ADVICE FOR MARRIED COUPLES

When engaging with your spouse, find out what gives them the most physical pleasure without violating your conscience. Sometimes you'll have to ask God for His wisdom and heart in the matter, but God is faithful to those who ask for wisdom. We need to combine agape love with eros love. Always remember that Paul told us to "Agape" our spouse in Ephesians 5:25: *"Husbands, love your wives, just as Christ also loved the church and gave Himself for her."*

I do believe most couples underestimate the importance and value of sexual love, allowing many things to pollute their hearts, and they miss out on this special blessing. We need to deal quickly with hurts and offenses so that our adversary cannot steal, kill, or destroy that precious love life with our spouse. We are all aware that aging does take its toll, and many older couples have resigned themselves to letting this part of their love spectrum fade out of their normal life. However, this doesn't mean that physical affection must also cease. Loving touches, hugs and kisses never need to cease, no matter how old we become.

Eros love is basically physical love. Phileo love, or brotherly love, is love that is on the level of the soul. Agape love, God's type of love, involves the human spirit responding to the Holy Spirit. These are the three most distinct kinds of love, and they are easily remembered because of the trichotomy of body, soul, and spirit. It could be said that the other five kinds of love are several varieties or combinations of soulish phileo love or perverted eros love. Full Spectrum Love that enriches and fulfills our lives, if we are in a committed marriage relationship, will involve the continuous development of these three primary forms of love. We need God's help to expand their development to reach a fuller potential. I won't say "fullest potential" because that implies we have exhausted that potential, and I don't believe we can ever exhaust our potential to grow in love.

Growing phileo-love friendships requires intentionality and determination, but mostly it requires God's help through the fruit and power of His Holy Spirit. In our book "The Marriage Anointing," we talk extensively about how spiritual fruit and gifts can be employed to conquer every marriage challenge. The same is true for all human relationships. We have been given an incredible toolbox full of supernatural power tools, but few people learn to use those tools, because they haven't read the instruction manual.

On the subject of Agape Love, let it suffice to say that there is only one reliable source for this most important kind of love. That source is ultimately the very heart of our Father in Heaven. God chose to love the crowning jewel of His creation with such sacrificial love that He gave His only begotten Son to die for us. Jesus paid the penalty for our numerous sins, so that fellowship could once again be restored with our Heavenly Father.

As believers and disciples of Jesus Christ, we have access to incredible resources. The most powerful resource of all is God's own Agape Love. When we allow that powerful and sacrificial love to flow through us into the hearts and lives of others, we can witness incredible miracles.

Not only can we bless multitudes of people through Agape Love, but we can also properly order our own lives in the following ways:

1. Individually, we are all first and foremost a spiritual being. Our spirit can interact and receive impartation from God's Holy Spirit.

2. We can direct and control the impulses of our soul (mind, will and emotions), so that they are in total alignment with God's Holy Spirit.

3. With our mind, will and emotions, we can then control our physical bodies to be in subjection to God's Holy Spirit.

It's God's Agape Love that has the power to regulate and align every other form of love given to us by our loving Heavenly Father. If we pursue this love more than anything else, we will be able to find solutions to almost every kind of problem we face. It will protect us from all kinds of deception, distraction, delusion, and enticement. In a later chapter, we will examine the power of a certain prayer that will help facilitate the practical power of Agape Love.

MOVING ON

Now that we have established that not all love is true love, or biblically righteous love, and we have encouraged you that sexual love is a special gift from God to enrich our lives, let's look at a very important aspect of Full Spectrum Love in our fallen world. This knowledge is critical if we want to fully enjoy and appreciate what God has given to us for our benefit.

CHAPTER THREE

MALE LOVE VS FEMALE LOVE

God is not a man, but neither is He a woman. When He created man, He gave him many of His own attributes, such as the desire to build, protect, provide, explore, defend, conquer, and administrate among other things. When He crafted a woman, He also gave her some of His most important attributes, which include showing compassion, nurturing, discerning, gentleness and serving. As we will emphasize, none of these character attributes are exclusive to one sex or the other, but some are usually the strongest in men and others are usually the strongest in women. A very simplistic way to look at it is that He made men with more physical strength and women with more emotional strength.

The important point is that God puts us together with different strengths and weaknesses. If we want to enjoy the benefits of Full Spectrum Love, we should listen to each other, learn from each other, and actually become more like each other. In doing so, we will actually become more like our God.

Brenda and I are about as different as night and day in our backgrounds, our giftings and our personalities, but we are very united in our calling and vision. I must admit that I've learned a huge amount about God by living with her for more than fifty-six years. The fact is that I seem to be more able now to understand, evaluate and assimilate the ways that she is different from me than ever before. I'm learning to stop comparing and mentally arguing why my way is better and allow her different perspective to upgrade my own to be more like God's and less like a macho male.

Remember that Jesus, who was the greatest human expression of the nature and character of God, manifested the positive traits of the male gender. He was also a man of emotion and sensitive to the needs of people, the same way that a typical female might be. Jesus was moved with compassion many times.

He wept over the city of Jerusalem and at the graveside of His friend Lazarus. He was concerned about how His disciples would handle His death and departure from the world. He instructed them and comforted them in John 14:1a saying, *"Let not your heart be troubled."* He also came as a servant and demonstrated that fact by washing the feet of His disciples. He was truly a masculine man, not at all effeminate, yet He was tender, gentle, kind and forgiving to the humble. He loved children in a very profound way, while He was rough and condemnatory toward the proud and super religious.

I love to teach and disciple those who want to be taught how to grow in their faith and walk with God. I want to build God's Kingdom by raising up disciples and equipping them to grow into maturity, so they can assist in building God's Kingdom on the earth. Brenda doesn't have the same passion to disciple with biblical truth. Her passion is to reveal God's love and power to heal and transform people by sharing His heart for them in words and actions.

Brenda loves to give gifts and speak encouraging words. She wants to bring healing and hope to the wounded and discouraged. She's all about revealing God's love and compassion. I'm not naturally into gift giving, and my words are usually more directive and corrective through teaching and by challenging disciples to be strong, courageous, and to never quit. I'm more like the football coach who has a passion to win and get the very best out of his players. Brenda is more like the doctor/trainer on the team who tries to get the wounded healthy again, and she encourages them that their career isn't over.

Is my gifting and calling better than Brenda's gifting and calling? Or are both equally needed? How ridiculous it would be to feel that one was more important than the other! This is what we must understand about Full Spectrum Love. The love of Jesus extended from the tough love towards his disciples, like a coach training His players to be the best they can be, to the gentle, kind, forgiving and tender-hearted lover of little children, as well as men and women caught in sin.

What I am learning now in my mid-to-late seventies is that God is teaching me through my spouse and other family members how to have a fuller-spectrum kind of love by becoming more like them. In doing so, I become much more like my Savior and my Heavenly Father. And what a blessing that is to me and my relationships with others!

Full Spectrum Love

Brenda often discerns things about people that I totally miss in my zeal to teach them what I know to help them become good disciples. She sees the need for healing and encouragement. Until those needs are addressed, my teaching is not going to produce any significant results in them. It's like in Psalm 23, until He restores (or heals) my soul, the Good Shepherd can't really lead me in paths of righteousness.

At the same time, if all the people receive is healing for their past wounds, they wouldn't mature and live the fulfilling lives that God intended in His Kingdom. Each person has a unique calling in life and role to play, just like the various roles that people can play on a North American football team. It's a sport that has a place for people of various builds and sizes. You can even be somewhat obese and still be an important part of a winning team. Likewise, God needs every unique individual on His team to do exploits together under His wise coaching.

CHAPTER FOUR

FULL SPECTRUM LOVE IN CREATION

One of my biggest passions of late has been to inform or remind people of the importance of God's creation, not just to us, but more importantly to Him. For His created beings to give credit for their very existence to a ridiculous theory that leaves Him out of the picture, is the ultimate insult and rejection. God has emotions, including anger, and I want to shout it from the rooftops that God does not take lightly such a blatant and offensive denial of His love as expressed in the magnificent creation He designed for our pleasure and prosperity.

God didn't need a universe filled with mystery and beauty for man to explore. He is eternal, outside of time and space. He created everything for humanity, fashioned in His own image. What an extreme insult to say we evolved through a series of millions of accidents over billions of years. It's as if Mother Nature and Father Time had partnered to create the entire universe in its vastness and complexity. For the purpose of this book, however, we want to focus on the incredible way that God's creation manifests His infinite and powerful Full Spectrum Love for us.

Psalm 19:1: *"The heavens declare the glory of God; and the firmament shows His handiwork."*

Just the word "glory" has a wide spectrum meaning that includes light, power, wealth, and above all, honor. Creation loudly and thoroughly declares these attributes of God. David, the shepherd who became king, was describing the sky and those bodies visible to the naked eye. He had no telescope to explore beyond what his human eyes perceived in the daytime or nighttime skies. And yet, the glory of what was visible was enough to cause him to marvel and write a psalm about it.

In complete agreement with King David, the Apostle Paul wrote the following: *"For the wrath of God is revealed from heaven against all ungodliness and unrighteousness of men, who suppress the truth in unrighteousness, because what may be known of God is manifest in them, for God has shown it to them. For since the creation of the world His invisible attributes are clearly seen, being understood by the things that are made, even His eternal power and Godhead, so that they are without excuse"* (Romans 1:18-20).

As we shared in an earlier paragraph, God does not take it lightly when men insult Him. Paul declares that God's wrath is revealed against sinners who don't respond to the obvious fact that there is a Creator who provided their beautiful home with all its incredible creativity-revealing features. In the next two verses that follow, Paul expands upon what men have done in order to justify the perversion of their hearts and minds, thus invoking the wrath of God.

Romans 1:21-22: *"Because, although they knew God, they did not glorify Him as God, nor were thankful, but became futile in their thoughts, and their foolish hearts were darkened. PROFESSING TO BE WISE, THEY BECAME FOOLS."*

Without getting into a discussion about the specific consequences of their turning away from God, let's just say, He was angry enough to virtually disown them, letting them do the things they wanted to do, which in the end brought their own self-inflicted punishment. It is biblically undeniable that God gets angry and severely punishes certain behaviors. These behaviors are rooted in the sin of pride, and they don't give God the credit He deserves for the gracious gifts and sacrifices He willingly made for us. Their pride led to rebellion, following the pattern set by their father, the devil.

The Ivy league of the Israeli education system in the days of Christ were the synagogues of the Pharisees. They were strict interpreters of their Mosaic constitution and system of laws, which they had added to with the wisdom of their rabbis. However, they had no understanding of the heart of their Creator. Like today's "woke" professors, they deemed themselves to be wise but became fools and had their Messiah crucified on a Roman cross - the greatest attack on the Godhead of all time. But in doing so, they also handed their "enemy" the greatest defeat of all time.

Because of this evil plan and the sinful hearts of the proud deniers of their own Creator, our Savior shed His blood so that the Father in Heaven could have a relationship with His beloved sons and daughters. The Son, our Savior, is able to look forward to a pure and spotless bride, who has washed her robes in His precious blood. The Holy Spirit also now has access to living temples that have been purified and overlaid with pure gold like Solomon's temple was in Jerusalem. The gold on those stones represented God's glory. Today, we can be clothed in His glory without the literal gold, but that glory is far more brilliant than any shiny metal could ever be.

BACK TO FULL SPECTRUM LOVE

Yes, God hates the denial of Himself as Creator by the fools who say in their hearts, *"There is no God"* (Psalm 53:1b). But He has a corresponding amount of love for those who exalt Him as Creator and stand strong in their proclamation of this aspect of Who He is - the Creator and sustainer of the universe and everything in it.

What I'm saying here is that if we want to increase God's favor and blessings in our lives, it would be very wise and prudent to acknowledge and thank Him as the brilliant designer of our most incredible world. I believe as we take a very brief look together at the infinite creativity revealed in God's creation, we will be honoring Him and invoking His favor. By making it our ongoing project to direct people's attention to the amazing artistry and creativity of God, we will draw His gracious blessings into our lives.

Perhaps that is one reason God so blessed the United States of America, whose founding fathers, led by Thomas Jefferson, declared that we were endowed by "Our Creator with certain unalienable rights." The Declaration of Independence also referred to "Nature's God." Nature is not sovereign, as implied in the concept of "Mother Nature." It all belongs to God. He has demonstrated His love towards us by providing an amazing universe with incredible beauty and vast resources. He gave us this beautiful planet to subdue and steward.

HOW DOES CREATION REVEAL FULL SPECTRUM LOVE?

From Microscopic To Telescopic:

God's love is unfathomable, His joy is unspeakable and full of glory, and His peace passes understanding. In other words, His gifts to us and His greatness cannot be described with earthly words. He demonstrates that truth through His creation at the microscopic and telescopic aspects of creation.

Full Spectrum Love In Creation

After six thousand years of recorded history, brilliant men are still trying to discover the infinite reaches of the tiniest particles that make up all living and non-living matter. At the same time scientists are exploring the farthest reaches of the universe, trying to discover how far it is to the most distant galaxies.

The incredibly vast difference in the sizes and distances involved in God's creation is a tremendous object lesson to describe Full Spectrum Love. You can't measure the smallest particles or the distance to the farthest galaxies and the stars within those galaxies. Additionally, there are many, many yet unsolved mysteries about the universe which should reinforce the fact that accidents, where nothing explodes into something, just don't create the order, beauty, and mystery as seen in our universe.

Let's look at a few numbers to wow us a bit. Of the scores of elements, all are made up of atoms, each containing a variety of infinitely tiny particles, such as electrons, protons, neutrons, and photons. Without trying to understand the size of these sub particles, let's just examine the size of the whole atom.

According to britannica.com, if you lined up fifty million atoms in a straight line, they would measure about one centimeter or less than half an inch in length. The article goes on to compare the relative size of the nucleus, which contains the protons and neutrons, to the size of the whole atom with its electron orbits. The size of just the nucleus of the atom compared to the size of the whole atom is like comparing the size of one marble to an entire football field.

According to the "Big Bang" theory, the universe was the result of several accidents. With the first big accident, a whole lot of "nothing" exploded in a "Big Bang" hurling fragments of "something" into the vastness of the universe. The particles from this explosion, composed of the tiniest things you could ever imagine joined and chemically bonded together to form the most massive celestial bodies filling the night sky with twinkling lights. How can we possibly imagine that these incredibly small particles, invisible to all but the most powerful microscopes, just happen to exist due to a series of accidents?

Without getting too technical with scientific terminology, we now turn to the vastness of God's created universe. Reading parts of the history of the attempts by scientists to measure the universe in astronomy.com, it became clear that there are many theories which cannot be confirmed. However, the writer of the article believes that they have already observed galaxies with high power telescopes as far as thirteen billion light years away from earth. One light year is equal to about six trillion miles. Thus, the radius of the known universe is thirteen billion times six trillion miles. This number written out would be 78,000,000,000,000,000,000,000. This number is way beyond my brain to imagine, but only God knows what is still beyond their ability to discover.

What an amazing illustration of God's Full Spectrum Love. From the tiniest particles of the atom to the incredible expanse of the universe, it is so absolutely true that *"The heavens declare the glory of God"* (Psalm 19:1).

CHAPTER FIVE

AWESOME RESULTS OF A FULL SPECTRUM PRAYER

In recent months I've been practicing and teaching a very special prayer that has truly produced wonderful results. It's the kind of prayer that God loves to answer because it's about His deepest desires. The focus of this prayer is on the person who is praying, not about someone we want God to change. The result is often that God does change the other person or persons, but the biggest change usually happens to the one who does the praying.

I've been calling this prayer the most important prayer you can pray once you're a believer. It's not a magic formula, because if you aren't praying with sincere motives, it won't produce the intended results. However, if you truly want God's best and desire to be a vessel He can use, this simple prayer can change you in ways you didn't think possible.

To test the power of this prayer on others, I issued a three-week challenge on social media. I asked people to commit to praying this simple prayer at least once a day for 21 days and then report the results. It was a volunteer response with no checking up on individuals who made the commitment. The results, however, were very rewarding. I will share a few testimonies later in this chapter.

Are you ready for the simple prayer we asked them to pray? It's simple, yet profound: *"Father, Give Me Your Heart!"*

Okay, so why is this such an important prayer and how does it relate to the subject of Full Spectrum Love? That's a great question and it has a very important answer.

THE HEART OF LOVE IS THE FATHER'S HEART!

Or putting it more plainly - the pure essence and the very source of all true love is the heart of our Heavenly Father. It has been correctly stated, in my opinion, that everything we see and have, came about because of the Father Heart of God. He longed for children whom He could bless by sharing His character and wisdom with them. Our magnificent universe was created by Full Spectrum Love for humanity. His interaction with Adam and Eve in the Garden was a precious expression of His love. His plan of redemption following their sin and rebellion was a tremendously sacrificial expression of His love. His plans for the Millennium and Eternity are uniquely powerful and awesome expressions of His Full Spectrum Love for His created beings, who so often lived in rebellion against their Eternal Father in Heaven.

God's Full Spectrum Love is always an expression of His Father's Heart for Humanity. His perpetual desire is to share the deepest desires of His heart with His eternal sons and daughters. Throughout God's Word, we are told that God looks on our hearts to discern our thoughts and motives. In II Chronicles 16:9, God said that His eyes *"run to and fro"* searching for hearts that please Him. David wisely requested God to search His heart to make sure that nothing was there except what pleased Him. God reminded Samuel, *"For the Lord does not see as man sees; for man looks at the outward appearance, but the Lord looks at the heart"* (1 Sam 16:7b).

The surest way to experience Full Spectrum Love is to experience and download the very source of love - the Father's Heart.

I believe we could safely say this: Every bad attitude and reaction to what happens to us in life is a result of NOT having the Father's Heart. So, let's get more practical. What are we actually talking about?

In addition to the basic five-word prayer *"Father, Give Me Your Heart,"* I suggested we add the little word "for" and then fill in the blank with someone's name. Thus, the prayer would look like this: *"Father, give me your heart for _____."*

The first name we usually need to add, if married, is the name of our spouse. The people we spend the most time with are usually the people who irritate us the most, because we don't see them with God's eyes.

More importantly, I believe, is the fact that we don't FEEL what God's heart feels for them. Yes, I'm talking about FEELINGS, and EMOTIONS. Our God is not an unemotional God. He is very much into emotions and not just intellectual thoughts and ideas. God feels deeply and reacts according to His feelings throughout the Bible. If you've been brainwashed into thinking that feelings are bad or not important to God, you need to read your Bible. It's everywhere from Genesis to Revelation. You might also want to check out our book, "Go Ahead, Be So Emotional."

So, when we're irritated with someone in our lives and feel angry or hurt by them, we can ask God to give us His heart for them. In other words, "When you see this person God, what are You feeling? Do You know something about them that I'm not aware of? Are they in pain and lashing out because of it? What is Your heart feeling that I'm not feeling?"

God is so ready and willing to share His heart with all who ask for it. There's nothing He values more than the privilege of sharing His heart with all who sincerely ask for it. As I'll share, it has changed a number of lives, besides my own.

PRACTICAL BENEFITS RECEIVED

Looking over the testimonies that I've received from people who accepted and followed through with the

"Prayer Challenge," I've seen many notable benefits to those who prayed this prayer.

1. **MARRIAGE HARMONY**

    Let me be the first to testify that this prayer has kept me from intensifying conflict and getting myself into trouble with wrong reactions. If Brenda says something that would naturally offend me, I ask God what He is feeling for my precious wife. He reminds me of physical and emotional pain that she's going through with various situations she's dealing with, as so many people share their pain with her compassionate heart. Instead of defending myself with a logical argument, I find myself asking her what she is going through at the moment that I'm not aware of. The marital conflict stops before it can start. At the same time, I've seen the results of Brenda praying this prayer for me. I've spontaneously said unthoughtful things, when I was physically or emotionally stressed, but she hasn't reacted the way she had a right to react. Instead, she has been calm and patient with me, allowing me the time to realize what I had done and to gain the good sense to apologize.

    Another married couple, named Bruce and Carole Robbins, both enthusiastically accepted the prayer challenge, and shared the results in great detail, which they had both faithfully journaled. I'm so grateful to them for their input. I'm sure the reader will also be challenged by what they shared.

Bruce shared a treasure-trove of benefits to his marriage that resulted from praying this simple prayer. Here are a few items from his journal, in which he is writing his thoughts to God:

"Murmuring – I have become aware that since I have been praying for the Father's heart for my wife, I have had less and less self-conversations or murmuring about instances that may happen between us. I have been able to move on from the experience quicker and the depth of things about the experience has lessened, if not disappeared. Essentially, I am murmuring less and extending more lovingkindness. This has resulted in a more joyful life for me and has affected the atmosphere of our home and relationship. Walking in joy and having Your peace has become a greater reality. Thanks. I love you."

"In the last couple of weeks, Carole and I have experienced a wonderful joy in our house. Even with some difficulties or misunderstandings, the Father's heart was revealed, and the joy of the Lord

became very evident. We both have been kinder to each other and have genuinely displayed pleasure in having each other's company. I like this. More Lord."

"I'm listening better. I'm more attentive - to Carole in particular. The Father's heart will help navigate the seasons of life we are in. It will help me focus on Carole – it already has. I love you, Lord."

Bruce sums up some of his insights:

"I've reread these notes on the Father's heart. It's challenged me to go deeper – to want more. You can't beat walking in His love. And pursuing His heart certainly causes one to want what is best for those you love. There has been a change in my heart for Carole in particular. I don't want this to stop growing and developing.

God has allowed me to experience pleasure in many things. I must admit nothing compares to Carole's smile as I love with the love I recognize as not of me, but from the Father. I am sure we are only scratching the surface in this. More of You and less of me is truly more as my less shifts into the unlimitedness of You, my Lord. I love you and thanks."

Carole Robbins adds a few thoughts regarding their marriage situations related to praying the Father's Heart prayer.

"I read Bruce's response to that 'dangerous prayer' and had to chuckle. He was the first one I asked the Father's heart for, and Bruce had obviously done the same for me. If couples would ask God to give them His heart for each other, it would result in stronger marriage bonds.

As far as the prayer for the Father's heart, I tend to be more emotional, while Bruce is steady. But then again, the tables can be turned, and I'll have to talk him through relationship issues with a hunting buddy, who happens to be a relative. What I've noticed is that when one of us shows our humanity, we can lean on the other, or pull the other out of the pit after a stumble. When the world is in chaos, we can walk in step with each other, rather than adding to the confusion around us. We make a stronger team when we are on the same page, sharing the love of the Father, and working together.

We've also become more sensitive to the needs of the other. When I'm working hard in the yard, for instance, Bruce will help me put the tools away when I'm done. He can't physically help weed the many gardens, which requires bending over for long periods, due to back issues. However, lending a helping hand when I'm exhausted is greatly appreciated. When he's doing repairs on the house, I try to return the favor and help him clean up the job site and put his tools away. He's very efficient, but I offer to help. I also try to maintain our home and provide a peaceful, comfortable environment, in spite of our two dogs. As we serve each other and think of small ways to please our spouse, the happiness factor increases. God will always provide the opportunity to fine tune our relationships. It's the little things that add up as we serve the Lord and each other."

2. **BUSINESS RELATIONSHIPS**

A business owner, named Mark Villegas, shared how he faced the trauma of selling his business and meeting a delegation of officials from the purchasing company. This situation would normally have been very stressful for him. However, he had begun to pray the Father's heart prayer, and he discovered an unbelievable calm and peace throughout the process. Following are some of his comments, starting with his first communication with me:

"I'm selling a large portion of my business. Yesterday was my closing day. This day has been a long time coming, and the build-up has been a lot to deal with. I strongly believe that the Lord has been guiding me in this direction. Although there has been nervousness and some anxiety for the unknown, I trust that this has been His direction in my life.

I began asking God for His heart when you first posted it. And yesterday, I cannot describe just how much peace I felt and how smoothly the closing went. However, our buyers are also staying for a month to learn and gather info, so yesterday and today have been jam-packed with nonstop tasks. This could have been enough to drive me crazy; but instead, I've had unsurpassed peace. Both days have been wonderfully pleasant. I told my office manager today about it all, and my only explanation to her was that Holy Spirit has been present and active. And I'm sure my addition of your specific prayer request to my prayers has been the difference."

In response to this testimony, I asked Mark the following questions:

(1) Did God help you see others through His eyes?

(2) Did you have more patience with people?

Mark's Response:

"I believe so on the first question. I've had multiple people taking over our office and roaming our warehouse. It had felt a little invasive, just because it has been my domain for decades and to just have people going through it all has been unsettling. But I have fairly quickly come to an acceptance of their behaviors. Each one, from their president to their CFO to all the others, I have been able to put myself in their shoes. I have found myself rising above the things I normally would expect myself to be irritated about. Instead, I began asking them questions in our short moments of down time about themselves, their families, their interests, etc. They have become more personable to me, and I've gained an understanding of how they must feel after traveling so far to be there and having paid their hard-earned money for a business.

The second question is a big YES! I've been very relaxed and patient with everyone It's really been surreal just how peaceful it has been."

One day later:

"I'm happy to report another amazing and consecutive day of peace. And today, we have had even more people from the buyer's company here. Thank you, Jesus!"

A few weeks later, Mark's final thoughts on the Father's Heart prayer.

"I would just like to add to my earlier testimony, that your prayer request has been so fruitful for me since the very beginning of praying it. It has somehow added a filter to my perception of others and to situations in my everyday life. The fruit that I have noticed the most is more compassion and patience for others. It has since been a daily staple in my prayer time. So, thank you again for putting this out there. It has been a gamechanger of sorts for me."

3. **FAMILY RELATIONSHIPS**

From Anonymous:

"Due to Covid, a wedding was delayed. A couple years later, when things began opening up, the wedding was rescheduled with the stipulation that all attendees must be vaccinated. The groom's parents wouldn't compromise their convictions and declined to take the vaccine as directed by the *bride's family of physicians, causing major consternation.*

A week before the wedding, the decision was reversed with a negative PCR test, and the groom's parents were allowed to attend. The wedding was a big, beautiful event, the guests were very joyous, but being rejected by the bride's family, with limited interaction during the event, greatly hurt the hearts of the groom's parents.

Two and a half years later, the groom's parents were suddenly informed that the same people who had rejected them had been invited by their son to Thanksgiving dinner at the home of a very close relative. The previously rejected couple fervently began praying the Father's Heart prayer in preparation for the encounter. When the bride's family walked in the front door, there were immediate smiles and hugs from them all around, even an invitation to their house in the future. Wow! That was so God and a miraculous turnaround! The couple was stunned and very thankful to God for answering their prayers. What seemed an impossible situation was possible with God!"

4. OTHER RESPONSES

From Cheryl, a Canadian friend, who calls herself Cher Bear:

"Asking daily and mostly in the morning, 'Father, give me Your heart for anyone I meet today.' It felt like a chore at first, but in a few days, I noticed that I was less offended while driving, more patient while waiting, and most of all, I felt love for people I didn't know. I saw their heart, and I often could feel their pain. It softened my heart, which I have kept guarded from the many wounds I have received myself. But I weep for those I do not know in a way that motivates my heart to remain open, no matter the arrows that come my way. I know the heart of the Father is my strength. When it comes to loving your enemies, I now have sadness for them, instead of anger. What an incredibly dangerous request it is to ask for the Father's heart, because you will change and desire to be more like Him. Thank you for the challenge."

From Carole Robbins:

"I think the first thing that impressed me was how BIG His heart is and how small mine is in comparison. I even found myself praying specifically for His heart in my sleep The needs are overwhelming around us daily. He needs to change our hearts first, so we can touch the hearts of others. I've found that I am kinder, and I listen more intently to others now. When we release His love and kindness, it comes right back to us! Let the love flow! So big, so small."

From Kim Adcock:

"Wow! Changed my perspective on so many things. Praying that prayer made me see others in a whole different light. I saw others now not only with compassion, but with unexplained empathy. To God be the glory! Great things He has done."

From another unnamed friend:

"I just spent five days with someone for whom I had prayed the Father's Heart Prayer. For the past eight years the relationship with this person has been a struggle for me. He has been a very special person in my life, but things had changed, and I regularly felt rejected, which was devastating to me. I tried for years to overcome this feeling. Then came the Father's Heart Prayer challenge. What had been nearly impossible to attain, changed for the good, almost overnight.

The time we recently spent together had a few moments of what would have been hard to take in the past. However, Holy Spirit enabled me to look right through those things and not be negatively affected. If anything, they strengthened my perspective of love and acceptance for my friend based upon my love acceptance by Jesus. The result was that I was not acting in a way that would facilitate love and acceptance for me, but instead I was genuinely interested in the well-being of my friend and the others with us. Consequently, we had a wonderful time together. I have been set free from the past hurts, and I am walking in a new freedom of thought that influences my loving, caring, and helpful acts of love towards my dear friend."

5. **ONE MORE IMPORTANT POINT**

You may not experience the full benefit of this point of access to Full Spectrum Love if you have not first prayed the Father's Heart Prayer for yourself. So, it would be wise, as you meditate on this chapter, that you pray that prayer and put your name in the blank. Maybe, God wants to tell you what He's feeling when He looks at you. It might be similar to what one of our friends heard God speak to her.

"Your heart pleases Me. Thank you for carrying My burdens and seeking My heart. You are a pleasing fragrance. I love you beyond comprehension. Share My love and walk in My great grace. Peace and love to all who will enter in. I love. I love with an overwhelming love. Bathe in it and share it. Freely have I given, freely give."

Then this friend added:

"His love is absolutely beyond comprehension! If we could only see ourselves through His eyes! There's no doubt about how much He loves us, but can we accept that overwhelming love? We need to pray the same prayer for ourselves as we do for others, 'Father, give me Your heart for me.' He will be faithful to do so."

It's time now to transition to an event that, more than anything else in history, demonstrates Full Spectrum Love. This event forever changed the future of the world and our eternal destiny.

CHAPTER SIX

THE PLAN, THE CROSS, AND THE BLOOD

THE PLAN

God was very determined to reveal His Full Spectrum Love to His creation. He devised a plan to demonstrate His love in such a way that it would be undeniable to anyone with an honest heart. That plan is summed up in John 3:16:

"For God SO LOVED the world that He gave His only begotten Son, that whoever believes in Him should not perish but have everlasting life."

How could God encapsulate, through one event, the length and breadth and depth of His Full Spectrum Love in a more powerful way than what He did through His Plan of Redemption? Consider the following facts:

1. God gave the single most valuable entity that He possessed, His only begotten Son, to show the extent of His love for man.

2. God sent the most honored, the most powerful, and the most beloved Being in all of Heaven to represent Him on earth.

3. Jesus, the very Creator of man and the entire universe, came from the most exalted position to be born in the most humble place possible - a manger.

4. Jesus spent His ministry doing good - healing the sick, cleansing the lepers, raising the dead, feeding the hungry, casting out demons, and teaching the poor.

5. Despite all His kindness and goodness, He suffered the greatest injustice from His own people, including the most honored leaders, as they judged and criticized Him for doing good deeds on the Sabbath Day.

6. Finally, He was nailed to a cross made from the wood He had originally created. He was mocked by both Herod's men (Jews) and Roman soldiers (Gentiles). He was humiliated and cursed by both exalted leaders and a wicked thief on a cross.

7. At the same time, Jesus asked the Father to forgive the soldiers who were parting His garments. When one of the thieves humbled himself and asked to be remembered when Jesus came into His Kingdom, He responded that he would be with Him in Paradise that day.

8. In laying down His life and suffering cruel torture, He was also carrying our sins in His body, becoming the sacrificial Lamb of God. Through His substitutionary atonement, He provided humanity with the opportunity to be forgiven, making our entrance into Heaven possible without any trace of our many sins.

9. His miraculous resurrection demonstrated the power of His love to overcome the things that His disciples would face.

10. His ascension into the clouds of Heaven demonstrated the fact that He had fulfilled His mission as the Son of Man to reveal God's Full

Spectrum Love. He was returning to His original position at the Father's right hand, but now with greater honor and authority than ever.

We could say a lot more about how God's redemption plan demonstrated Full Spectrum Love, but let's focus on the symbol of the cross itself.

THE CROSS

The very shape of the cross speaks volumes to me about Full Spectrum Love.

Jesus' head was pointing up toward Heaven. He continually spent time with His Father to receive wisdom and direction for His walk on the earth. Jesus shared in John 5:19 that the Son only does what He's seen His Father do. I believe His times alone with God in the night were when His Father would prepare Him for the next day.

Jesus' feet were pointing toward the earth. His mission was to bring the Father's love from Heaven above to the earth beneath. He had done this for thirty-three years, and now on the cross, His mission was illustrated in such a powerful way.

Jesus' arms were stretched out in both directions, symbolically embracing the world. It's another example of Full Spectrum Love, as a full embrace is like a ring that has no end. His arms represent His love, His comfort, and His labor of love to heal and set the captives free from Satan's grasp.

In another picture of Full Spectrum Love, we can see how the cross represented total humiliation and torment. While on the other hand, it was prophetic of the throne that Jesus would be positioned on. When that takes place, His hands will be free to wield the scepter of justice and His feet will be free to walk among His people, leading them wherever He wants them to go.

Jesus wore a cruel and painful crown of thorns on His head, which was prophetic of the royal crown He will wear during the greatest coronation ever held on the earth.

On the cross, Jesus was stripped of His clothing. On His Heavenly throne, He will have the most glorious royal robes ever worn by any man. What an amazing picture of Full Spectrum Love!

THE BLOOD

The essence of life is found in the blood. Before the current scientific era with today's powerful microscopes, humans didn't know much about the dozens of elements on the periodic scale that scientists now work with every day. They didn't know about hydrogen, nitrogen, carbon, helium, etc. They didn't know anything about oxygen, the specific element humanity can't live without. But still, they knew that "life was in the blood." They also knew that life was in the breath or spirit of man. Somehow, the breath and the blood were tied together. They both represented "life" to the Jewish people. To me, they both represent the work of the Holy Spirit. He IS the breath of eternal life, and He moves throughout the Body of Christ, bringing that life to every organ and cell.

The Old Testament Law revealed a great reverence for blood. The Law of Moses required that the Children of Israel pour out the blood of the animals they were going to eat. They were not to eat meat cooked in the blood, due to the reverence for the life that it represented. At the same time, blood sacrifices were required to cover the sins of men. Blood was a significant part of the sacrifice and in any covenants made between man and God. The blood of a spotless lamb was sprinkled on the Mercy Seat in the Holy of Holies by the High Priest, who was a descendent of Aaron.

And, of course, we know that Jesus is our Sacrificial Lamb. For all who receive the free gift of salvation, He's the pure and spotless Lamb that takes away the sins of the world. It is His blood, and only His blood, that can cover our sins and cleanse our hearts of all iniquity.

Let's take a closer look at the composition and function of our blood and see how it also demonstrates Full Spectrum Love. The information below was gathered from various internet sites.

1. **PLASMA**

    This is the liquid component of your blood that makes up about 55% of your blood's total volume. Plasma helps your body recover from injury, distributes nutrients, removes waste, and prevents infection, while moving through your circulatory system.

    The blood of Jesus accomplishes similar things in our lives and should be applied frequently throughout the day.

2. **RED BLOOD CELLS**

    The red blood cells are the ones that bring oxygen to the tissues in your body and release carbon dioxide to your lungs for you to exhale. Oxygen turns into energy, which is an essential function to keep your body healthy.

This especially speaks of the work of the Holy Spirit, bringing life to our bodies and to the Body of Christ.

3. **WHITE BLOOD CELLS**

The job of white blood cells is to fight infections and cancers. They also remove poison, waste, and damaged cells from the body. The number of white cells increase when the body is fighting infection or disease and decrease when a person is healthy.

We need these fighters contained in the blood of Jesus, to deal with the infections of sin and spiritual cancers in our lives. The white speaks of purity and the purification of our soul.

4. **PLATELETS**

The platelets get their name from their appearance as little, microscopic plates. Their function is to form clots and stop the bleeding when injured. They do this by rushing to the injury site and growing sticky tenacles that adhere to one another, forming the blood clot that keeps the rest of the blood from flowing out of the body.

Once again, we see the work of the blood of Jesus in stopping the bleeding when we are ready to bleed out and give up on life. It's all in the blood of Jesus.

What an amazing illustration of Full Spectrum Love God gave us when He created the blood. Every part of the blood is essential and has an important function for us to survive. When people suffer from either too many or too few vital blood components, they can become sick or even die. We need the full spectrum of blood to remain healthy.

We need the Holy Spirit to breathe life into every part of the Body of Christ. Within the church body, we need to identify those who are the peacemakers, prayer warriors and healers, so they can function as the various aspects of the blood:

- The red blood cells (Holy Spirit) carry oxygen to the body, release carbon dioxide in the lungs, and provide energy.

- The plasma (peacemakers) keeps everything flowing together. It distributes nutrients, removes waste, helps with recovery, and prevents infection.

- The white blood cells (prayer warriors) fight cancers and infections in His body.

- The platelets (healers) stop the bleeding as quickly as possible.

The different parts of the body can team up and work together when they need to get the job done. The sum of the various components of our blood displays a beautiful picture of Full Spectrum Love.

May we all, as members of Christ's body, remember how important it is that we support and assist one another, while not forgetting our own responsibilities and assignments. And may we forever be thankful for the precious blood Jesus shed for us to demonstrate to the whole world the wonders of Full Spectrum Love.

CHAPTER SEVEN

FULL SPECTRUM ROMANCE

In this final chapter, we'd like to put the ribbon and bow on this Valentine's Day package and share some thoughts about the subject of romance from a Full Spectrum Love perspective.

DATING AND ROMANCE

Many years ago, in my college days, I read a book called "Unto Full Stature" by DeVern Fromke, which greatly impacted my understanding of love. One chapter was titled "Should a Christian Fall in Love?"

This was a very intriguing title, since most of my friends, along with myself, were into some serious romances at the time.

Fromke's answer was, "No, a Christian should not fall in love. A Christian should rise or grow in love." He pointed out the three common Greek words for love, which we discussed earlier. He described "falling in love" as the picture of our love going from Agape Love to Phileo Love to Eros Love. He saw the results of young men and women submitting to the forces of Eros Love, where this lower level of love was in control, rather than Agape Love.

He was not saying physical love was evil, but He was saying it should not be in charge of our actions or our lives. He advocated a healthy spiritual love being in control and having the power to overrule the passions of physical attraction and sexual activity.

WESTERN ROMANCE VS EASTERN ROMANCE

Most of us have grown up with the culture of the west that promotes the concept of the "falling in love" kind of romance. We have little knowledge of the Eastern World culture that involves the parental control of the marriage of their sons and daughters. The very thought of such a thing causes our western minds to recoil in disgust at such a thought.

In my international travels, I remember discussing with a young Asian man his concerns about whom he would marry. His parents had selected a certain girl, but there were some concerns, and his parents were investigating further. He had some input into their decision, but they were all concerned that it would be a good, practical decision. In reality, it was more like a business decision as to what kind of girl would be a good match and a blessing to their son.

In their culture they were not even thinking about marrying whoever one fell in love with. It was assumed that you would make it work once you had signed the wedding covenant. And most couples did make it work because that's what their culture demanded.

Of course, we know that the Jewish culture and the culture of other Middle Eastern people groups are more in harmony with the East than the West. The Bible was written by men of the East who shared the Eastern concepts.

However, we do have some mixture of the East and West in some of the Bible stories. Abraham did send his servant to find a wife for Isaac, as per the Eastern culture. However, we find Jacob, who was far from home, falling in love with Rachel, but first marrying Leah, whom he didn't love, before serving another seven years for Rachel. We also have the story of Sampson, who asked his parents to get him a Philistine woman that he had met and fallen in love with.

Thus, even though the culture said the parents were in charge of whom they married, there was such a thing as falling in love and finding a way to marry that person.

WISDOM FOR ROMANCE AND MARRIAGE TODAY IN OUR CULTURE

With the above discussion in mind, what makes sense for young as well as older couples today when it comes to romance and marriage as well as love after marriage?

There's no doubt that both the Western and Eastern cultures have serious problems to deal with. We know that in the Eastern culture, people may have to live together without the blessings of that "wow factor" that we in the west value so highly. It's the thrill of looking in each other's eyes, catching those special glances of admiration and care and wondering if he or she really likes me. It's the wonderful feeling of holding hands walking through a park, enjoying God's creation together. It's the thrill of that first kiss and holding your partner close. It's dreaming of being intimate and loving each other with Full Spectrum Love on every level. The Eastern culture cares little for such intangibles that Westerners highly esteem.

We also see how many people in the West have been convinced that they have found their one true love, with all of the above in place. They just know that they will live happily ever after, only to discover after marriage that their perfect soulmate does many things that totally irritate them. Their flesh rises up and they swear their spouse is no longer the person they married, requiring them to separate or divorce.

I, personally, was extremely blessed as a young man to have experienced a powerful and intimate extended season of personal revival before getting to know this cute girl in Bible College named Brenda Pinkerton. I was honestly in a place where I was controlled by Agape Love in such a way that God had given me His heart for souls and revival for everyone I encountered. It was an interesting story and set of circumstances that led us together. For several months, as we got to know each other, I believe that God had given me a perfect balance of Full Spectrum Love, which was exactly what my Brenda needed from me, coming from a very difficult home situation. She didn't need a guy who was just interested in what she could provide for him. God filled me with His Agape Love, and I became an intercessor for her, not knowing at the time that she would become my wife. God gave me a passion to minister to her through the Scripture that He kept giving me for her.

As time went on, God began to confirm to me that Brenda was indeed the one. During these first months of brief encounters, allowed by the Bible College, we had no physical contact. I shared my excitement about the power of prayer and the passion for revival that God had given me. I read Scripture to her and prayed with her. Brenda was excited to be with someone that cared more about helping her than wanting to get something from her. She was also hungry for a touch from God, and I was blessed to be her mentor as an eighteen/nineteen-year-old.

And yes, I was romantically drawn to this lovely young lady, as I admired her beauty and her vibrant personality, along with her amazing unselfishness and concern for others. I was fully in awe of her and in Full Spectrum Love with her. She never wanted me to spend money on her, knowing my resources were extremely limited. I was frankly not intimidated by my lack of finances. I knew I had something much more important, which was my relationship and faith in a powerful, miracle-working God who provided for my every need.

I know my testimony is highly unusual. As I shared, I was extremely blessed with the timing of God in my life. I wasn't looking for a girl to meet my needs like most young men my age with naturally active hormones were. My soul was totally satisfied with my daily intimate time with God, and He had given me total victory over sensual desires that had plagued me as a youth. It was an incredible miracle, and you can read about it in some of my other books, such as "Humility and How I Almost Achieved It."

Of course, I recommend that everyone have a similar personal revival. But being realistic, the following are a few suggestions.

1. Let's blend some of the best of the East with the best of the West.

2. We need to position ourselves to be the bride that the Father is searching for to present to His Son. Our first loyalty should be to our future Bridegroom. We should walk in purity, knowing that He is preparing to give us garments of white for our wedding ceremony.

3. Wisdom should be used to gain some practical advice from parents, grandparents, and wise friends, rather than from our peers who may actually know less than we do.

4. Above all, get confirmation from the Holy Spirit through His Word. My decisions are always based on Scriptures that the Holy Spirit highlights when I read them. Those decisions included my education direction and marriage timing.

5. Enjoy getting to know people in a safe setting. Pray earnestly that you would be ruled by Agape Love, not Eros Love. Recognize your need for words of affirmation, and don't be drawn into a relationship because someone knows what words you long to hear.

6. Don't compromise for fear of losing someone. If they walk away when you stand firm, they may have just saved you from a disaster-filled future.

7. Ask yourself, "Is this the person God wants me to minister to for the rest of my life?" Don't ask, "Is this the person who will make me happy?" That's a sure recipe for unhappiness.

8. Financial stability or security may be important, but it won't bring the fulfillment your soul desires.

9. Do you have compatible visions that will enable you to support each other in the projects you undertake?

10. Do you have the humility necessary to go for counseling if difficulties arise? Do you know qualified people who can help you undertake a marriage journey?

If you are a Westerner, like me, I encourage you to enjoy courtship, but only with the help and guidance of the Holy Spirit. Ask Him for Full Spectrum Love. Ask Him to help you live from an Agape-dominated relationship.

ALREADY MARRIED?

Happily, most of the principles of romance and dating can apply to married couples as well. It's just a matter of some minor adjustments. We certainly need to keep the romance alive long after the wedding, and that will certainly happen if we pursue Full Spectrum Love in our marriage. For further marriage wisdom, please check out our book "The Marriage Anointing."

Most importantly, put your greatest focus on intimacy with God, rather than with a potential life-partner. Otherwise, you may experience a lot of relationship problems and heartache in the future. It all starts with having the Father's heart.

FINAL SUMMARY

We've covered a lot of ground regarding Full Spectrum Love. I found it to be a very fascinating concept as I did research for this Valentine's Day special. But why exactly is it so important to God for us to understand and pursue this concept of love? Let's list a few key answers to that question.

WHY WE NEED TO PURSUE FULL SPECTRUM LOVE

1. Full Spectrum Love will deliver us from religion and the religious spirit. We won't be satisfied with rules and legalism if we have tasted the fullness of God's love.

2. Full Spectrum Love flowing through us will win the lost to Christ. God's Agape love, when presented in its purity and power, is irresistible to those who are seeking the truth and who haven't already sold out to the enemy.

3. Full Spectrum Love, when received in its fullness, will heal the hurts in our soul and give us a wholesome attitude toward life and those in our lives.

4. Full Spectrum Love gives us a heart to receive as well as manifest all the fruit of the Holy Spirit. It also enables us to properly employ the powerful gifts the Holy Spirit has given us.

5. Full Spectrum Love will make our marriages and other relationships so much more fulfilling and blessed. I thank God for blessing me so richly with His Full Spectrum love.

THE BIG QUESTION

I believe Jesus wants to use this book as His personal Valentine's card to you. I trust you have been completely convinced that His love for you is totally Full Spectrum Love, and there's nothing artificial about it. He is your Sunshine and His love lights up your life. And now, with this very special Valentine's card, He's asking you, His most precious creation, "WILL YOU BE MY VALENTINE?"

PRAYER FOR BELIEVERS

Heavenly Father, I'm so thankful for the incredible way You chose to demonstrate Your Full Spectrum Love to Your children. I'm sorry I haven't been as grateful as Your amazing sacrifice deserves. I'm asking You to help me pursue the Full Spectrum Love that You have so graciously provided for me.

I want to receive Your love so I can be healed and made whole, enabling me to pass this powerful blessing onto others. Show me daily where I am walking in a lesser form of love and manifesting my own flesh instead of Your Agape love. Thank You again for paying that price for me. I want to experience the full potential that You have provided for me to bring glory to Your name and to help expand Your Kingdom. In the powerful and holy name of Jesus Christ, our Savior and Lord. Amen!

PRAYER FOR SEEKERS WHO HAVE NEVER INVITED JESUS TO BE THEIR SAVIOR

Heavenly Father, thank you for demonstrating Your love to me by sending Jesus to die for me, which enabled me to be free from the power and penalty of my sins against You. I receive the forgiveness You have

Full Spectrum Love

provided for me. I am very sorry for living selfishly and not receiving Your love before this time.

I've never really understood how much You loved me. I've been hurt, even by people who claimed to be Christians. But I know that it wasn't Your will for me to be hurt, and You are giving me the power to forgive each one. Please come into my life and change my heart. I surrender control of my destiny and plans to You. You know what's best for me and I want to serve You for the rest of my life. Thank you for receiving me as Your child. Please help me grow and become a mature person that You can use to bring Your good news to others. In Jesus' name, Amen!

Full Spectrum Love
Is The Key!

About Ben R. Peters

Ben R. Peters has been a student of the Word since he could read it for himself. He has a heritage of grandparents and parents who lived by faith and taught him the value of faith. That faith produced many miracle answers to prayer in their family life, as Ben and his wife, Brenda, have shared over 55 years of marriage and gospel ministry. Together they founded Kingdom Sending Center, in northern Illinois, and travel extensively, teaching and ministering prophetically to thousands each year. Their books are available on most e-readers, all other normal book outlets, as well as their website:

www.kingdomsendingcenter.org

Other Books Written by Ben R. Peters

1. A Mandate to Laugh
2. Birthing the Book Within You
3. The Boaz Blessing
4. Catching Up to the Third World
5. **Christmas Future – New!**
6. Cinco Ministeriors En Un Poderoso Equipo
7. Faith on Fire
8. Finding Your Place on Your Kingdom Mountain
9. Folding Five Ministries into One Powerful Team
10. God is So God!
11. God's Favorite Number
12. Go Ahead, Be So Emotional
13. Holy How?
14. Holy Passion – Desire on Fire
15. Humility and How I Almost Achieved It
16. The Kingdom-Building Church
17. Kings & Kingdoms
18. **The Glorious Return of King Jesus – New!**
19. The Marriage Anointing
20. Ministry Foundations 101
21. Prophetic Ministry -Strategic Key to the Harvest
22. Resurrection! A Manual for Raising the Dead

Other Books Written by Ben R. Peters (Continued)

23. *Signs and Wonders - To Seek or Not to Seek*
24. *The Ultimate Convergence*
25. *Veggie Village and the Great & Dangerous Jungle*
26. *With Me*

A Mandate to Laugh

Overcoming the Sennacherib Spirit

In this book you will learn about the demonic power that possessed Sennacherib and how it is influencing our society and political powers today. The clear and sinister purpose of the Sennacherib spirit is to control all people and nations for personal glory, power, and profit. Yet, there is still hope God is not finished with the world!

Birthing the Book Within You

Inspiration and Practical Help to Produce Your Own Book

Writing and publishing your own book has never been easier, thanks to computer and digital printing technology. Ben R. Peters has been down this road many times, and now in this book, he shows how you can do it too. With spiritual insight and inspiration, he offers many practical tips to help you give birth to the book within you.

The Boaz Blessing

Releasing the Power of This Ancient Blessing Into Your World Today

The Boaz Blessing will give you courage as you dare to believe for the favor of God for yourself, for the people you love, and for the people who need to understand the mercy of their heavenly Father.

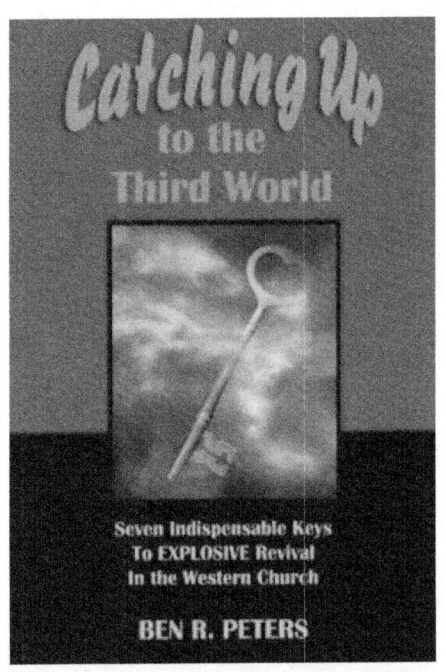

Catching Up to the Third World

Seven Indispensable Keys to Explosive Revival in the Western Church

Catching Up to the Third World reveals how God is provoking the Western Church to godly jealousy, to produce a powerful revival in the "First World" nations, so that the resources of the West can be most effectively utilized in the coming global harvest.

Ben's Newest Book!

Christmas Future

Good News of Great Joy!

Was Christmas Past Prophetic of a Christmas Future? Will angels appear again to shepherds? Will wise men seek to encounter Jesus again? Be prepared for some surprises as Ben R. Peters predicts an amazing Christmas Future event leading up to the Really Really Big Event.

Cinco Ministerios En Un Poderoso Equipo

Llevando la Reforma Profetica y Apostolica Al Siguiente Nivel

Este libro da a la iglesia una visión de lo que podemos lograr cuando capacitamos a cada ministerio para hacer lo que mejor puede hacer como parte del equipo ministerial que Dios ha dado a la iglesia.

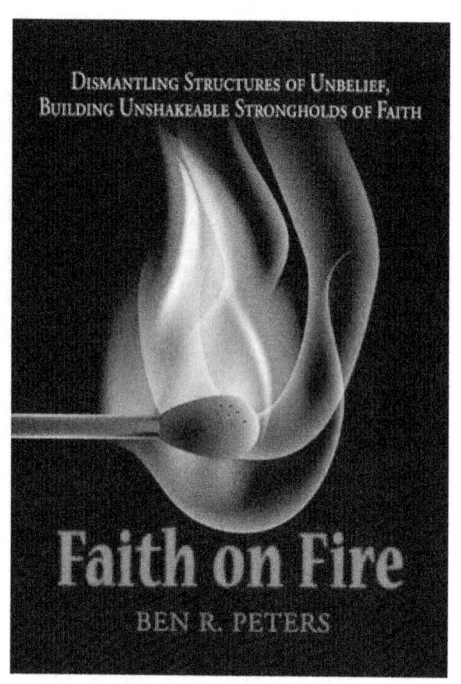

Faith on Fire

Dismantling Structures of Unbelief, Building Unshakeable Strongholds of Faith

Most Christians wonder why they don't see greater results from their prayers. In *Faith on Fire*, Ben R. Peters addresses these questions and identifies the structures of unbelief that may be keeping you in fear, doubt, and insecurity.

Finding Your Place on Your Kingdom Mountain

A Practical Guide and Workbook for Reigning as Kings in the Kingdom of God

In *Finding Your Place on Your Kingdom Mountain,* Ben R. Peters gives you practical help to discover on which of the "Seven Mountains" of society God wants you to display the rule and reign of His kingdom.

Folding Five Ministries into One Powerful Team

Taking the Apostolic and Prophetic Reformation to the Next Powerful Level

This book gives the Church a vision for what can be accomplished when we empower each ministry to do what it does best as part of the ministry team that God has given to the Church.

God is So God!

The Adventures of a Traveling Ministry on a Prophetic Faith Journey

Brenda Peters knows what it's like to launch out on a faith journey with only an RV for her home. This book, filled with her road adventures in a full-time traveling ministry, reveals the awesome power of God to intervene in every aspect of life. This is a unique book, full of faith stories and prophetic adventures that will touch your heart.

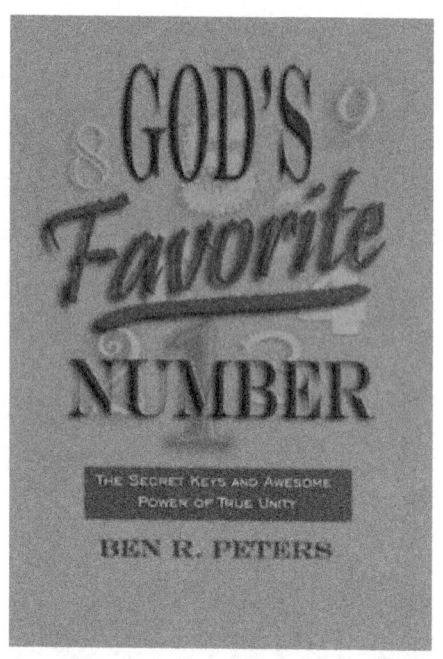

God's Favorite Number

The Secret Keys and Awesome Power of True Unity

Does God have a favorite number? Yes, He does - so much so that you'll find it 1,969 times in Scripture. It's a number that relates to unity.

Go Ahead, Be So Emotional

Empowering the Emotional Personality To do Awesome Exploits for God

It's time for all of God's emotionally expressive people to rise up and fulfill their destiny. In this book you will learn how to let the anointing of God come upon you as you use your emotional personality to take more territory for His kingdom.

Holy How?

Holiness, the Sabbath, Communion and Baptism

Enjoy the Privilege of Being Holy to the Lord! Believer, you are chosen to be special and unique and filled with the very nature of God, through your intimate relationship with the Father, Son, and Holy Spirit.

Holy Passion – Desire on Fire

Igniting The Torch of Godly Passion

God is a God of passion, and He is looking for a people with passion!

Humility and How I Almost Achieved It

UNCOVER A HIGHLY UNDERVALUED KEY TO LASTING SUCCESS AND KINGDOM POWER! You will learn the greatest shortcut to true humility, plus some practical ways to stay humble about being humble.

The Kingdom-Building Church

Experiencing the Explosive Potential of the Church in Kingdom-Building Mode

Come with Ben R. Peters and explore what the heart of God cries out for, what the plans of God are for His church, and what He can do when we allow Him to put us in Kingdom-building mode.

Kings and Kingdoms

Anointing A New Generation of Kings to Serve the King of Kings

In *Kings and Kingdoms*, Ben R. Peters explores what it means to be a king under the authority of Jesus Christ and how you can truly "seek first the Kingdom of God" by fulfilling your role as king over the domain God has given you.

New Book!

The Glorious Return of King Jesus

The Rapture and The Great Tribulation

Is there biblical evidence for a rapture? Is "Left Behind" an actual scriptural concept? Did God give us a type and shadow of His second coming in His Holy Word? This concise and easy-to-read investigation leaves little doubt what the answers to these and other questions are. You will love this unique journey!

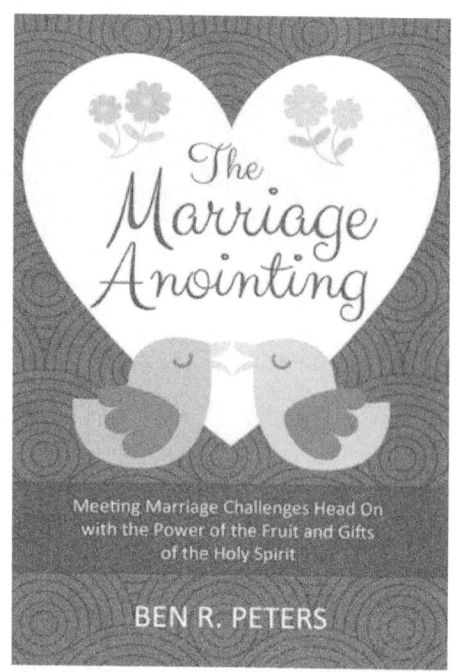

The Marriage Anointing

Meeting Marriage Challenges Head on With the Power of the Fruit and Gifts of the Holy Spirit

Meet your marriage challenges head on! There is no power from hell that can defeat *two* people who have learned to listen to God's voice and invite Him to bless them with everything He wants to bestow upon them. This book shows you how, with the "double-barreled" approach of the Fruit and Gifts of the Holy Spirit, your marriage can become a huge source of fulfillment for both partners and together become an awesome ministry team.

Ministry Foundations 101

Preparing the Saints for the Work of the Ministry

The goal of this study is to help you be the best possible stewards of the gifts, talents, knowledge, and experience that God has given to each of you.

Prophetic Ministry

Strategic Key to the Harvest

Ben R. Peters knows from first-hand experience the value and effectiveness of prophetic ministry as an evangelistic tool. Along with his wife Brenda, he has been doing prophetic ministry since 1999. He has seen countless salvations, healings, and miracles as a result.

Resurrection

A Manual for Raising the Dead

Let's Raise the Dead! Raising the dead is not for super-Christians but is in the DNA of every believer.

Signs and Wonders
To Seek or Not to Seek

Exploring The Power of the Miraculous to Bring People to Christ

To Seek or Not to Seek? Signs and Wonders gives a clear and resounding answer to that controversial question. The conclusions of this thorough and fascinating investigation of the faith-making power of the miraculous will be difficult to refute.

The Ultimate Convergence

An End Times Prophecy of the Greatest Shock and Awe Display Ever to Hit Planet Earth

Convergence has been a hot buzzword in Kingdom streams for the past few years. Ben R. Peters believes that God is preparing for the greatest convergence of natural and spiritual elements of all time in preparation for His great harvest and the coming back to earth of His Beloved Son, Jesus Christ.

Veggie Village and the Great & Dangerous Jungle: An Allegory

When church becomes more of a religion than a relationship, it can seem like just eating our vegetables. We are told to do good things like read our Bibles, pray, and go to church because they are good for us - and they are. However, God wants to win the lost, and it is often not easy to get others to come and eat with us if we offer only vegetables.

With Me

With Me takes you on an incredible journey of discovery about the Lord Jesus, as it uncovers a refreshing new revelation from the most famous Psalm in Scripture.

All Books are available on Amazon and through
Kingdom Sending Center
www.kingdomsendingcenter.org

Printed in Great Britain
by Amazon